ZANATEK

Barbara-Ann McCarthy

BALBOA.
PRESS
A DIVISION OF HAY HOUSE

Balboa Press books may be ordered through booksellers or by contacting:

Balboa Press
A Division of Hay House
1663 Liberty Drive
Bloomington, IN 47403
www.balboapress.com.au
1 (877) 407-4847

Print information available on the last page.

ISBN: 978-1-5043-1731-3 (sc)
ISBN: 978-1-5043-1732-0 (e)

Balboa Press rev. date: 03/26/2019

To my husband John and my childen, Sarah and Simon.

Enjoy the journey.

CONTENTS

PREFACE

When I first started writing *Zanatek*, the world was in a constant state of flux – the World Trade Center Terror attacks had occurred, the environment continued to deteriorate and the rise of Al Qaeda and ISIS – was terrifying to behold.

I sought to address these and other distressing occurrences, and to come to terms with all the terrible events that continue to take place in this world of ours, by creating worlds and species of my own.

ONE

AND SO IT BEGINS

No one had ever seen anything like it. The skies were ablaze with streaming lights, and sparks emanated from what looked like comets. Everyone was amazed at such an impressive sight, but then amazement turned to horror as they realized that these comets were coming right towards them…

⌘ ⌘ ⌘

The blazing suns beat down unmercifully on the workers as they toiled the fields, hoping that this crop would survive the cruel winter. It was the year 8053. Last year's produce had been inedible, and many of Uuffi's people had died because they couldn't to eat it. 'But surely this year's will be better?' Uuffi thought to himself, as he toiled along with them. 'Surely this year the Gods will be merciful!' But how was he going to face his people if they were not? And still the sun became stronger. His parched throat ached as did his heart for his starving people. This was a planet of extreme temperatures, and it had no mercy for those who could not stand up to its capriciousness.

✄   ✄   ✄

Malcolm Xenides strolled thoughtfully up and down his luxurious office, which was located on the 488th floor of Zanatek. He had worked long and hard to be where he was now, and had sacrificed many on his way, including his family, for whom he had never had time, and who no-longer regarded him as having a part in their lives. He was eighty-eight years old, but because of all the technological and scientific breakthroughs, he was only considered to be middle-aged. The longest known living person now was 253, very different from the old days of 2018, when life was not expected to exceed the early 100s. 'I could easily work for at least another 100 years if not longer, if I look after myself well,' the Top Scientific Corporate Director thought as he viewed himself with approval in the mirror of his executive bathroom.

Tall and solidly built, with sandy hair and blue eyes, he looked very good for his age, having grown up with the very best food and technology available.

Zanatek was the largest Scientific Corporate Company in the known universe – a Conglomerate. It was practically a planet on its own, and very successful.

Malcolm's thoughts were interrupted by his personal assistant entering the room. She was of medium height, with black wavy hair and brown eyes, 'Quite stunning to look at,' Malcolm had thought on many occasions when she was speaking to him.

"I've processed all those file discs that you wanted me to process," the young P.A. said breathlessly, "so everything should be all right now, shouldn't it?"

"Yes. Don't worry about a thing, Wandana," he said reassuringly, reluctantly releasing his gaze from the mirror. "You are much too young to be worried about what is going on here".

"Ok," the young girl said. But was not convinced as she was expertly ushered out of the office.

Alone with his thoughts again, Malcolm began straightening up his office to prevent him from thinking about the inevitable. This place was going to hell in a handbasket, and he knew that he, and he alone, was to blame. He was the one who had made the big decisions as to where this company was now headed, and now he was the one who must take responsibility for the chaos that was on the planet Trixis. People where dying there and other planets, from some previously-unknown disease. ' It's unfortunate but it couldn't be helped,' he mused to himself. How could I have predicted such an outcome from my decisions?' After all, he was no rocket -scientist ; he was just trying to run a company.

Wandana Galantez made her way home on the inter-galactic shuttle. She hoped the other passengers couldn't detect her rising sense of panic. Sure, Malcolm Xenides had been reassuring and seemed very confident about what was going on and what was about to happen. Still, she could not convince herself that everything was going to be alright. People were dying on her planet, and she could do nothing but watch it happen. Wandana hated feeling helpless; that was not the way her father had brought her up on Trixis. The eldest of five children, she was the one her father and mother had depended on to get an education and better herself. "So that you will have a life filled with hope," they had said. "Not one of despair and wretchedness, as we are now living.

Once, Trixis was thriving. Many beings from other planets had visited to swim in the beautiful oceans and walk along its sun-soaked beaches of this purple planet. They came to see the unusual flora and fauna, and to meet the amiable Trixians. But that was before the climate began to change. With the event of the increasingly hotter springs and summers, and more unrelentingly cold autumns and winters the mainstay of their economy, namely produce, had been drastically reduced, and the Trixians were reduced to living on meagre wages, and sustaining themselves on whatever crops could still be cultivated.

'If Wandana could get away from here and learn the new ways,' Talanta and Uuffi had thought, 'she could save us all.' They had heard of the people who lived on Zanthium, and worked for the company Zanatek, and all the wonderful things they had achieved. They had heard that these people could live as long as 250, as opposed to only 100 on Trixis.

Wandana's parents had toiled hard in the fields and sold well in the market-place, so that their oldest child could study at the prestigious Polanta University on the planet Zanthium, and after graduating, she had acquired a prestigious position of personal assistant to Malcolm Xenides, the managing director at Zanatek no less!

'And now, everything that my mother, father, and all our people have worked for, for so many years is falling apart,' she thought to herself miserably. 'I have failed!' 'How can I face them?' 'Stop this!' she admonished herself. 'Stop feeling sorry for yourself. You know what you have to do. You must warn your people of what is about to happen, so that at least this way they might have a chance to survive!' And with that, she

TWO

ZANATEK

Malcolm Xenides had called an urgent meeting with his most trusted senior staff members. He wasn't going to take all the blame himself he decided. After all, though he had presided over all meetings, these executives had attended, and had voted unanimously on the motions that had been raised. He had made sure of that. He had also made sure that he had members of the more educated of the different species of the galaxy represented on the Board of Directors, as well as Terrarians.

Bill Osmond was the first to arrive, nervously fiddling with the Zanatek badge on his jacket lapel. All the employees who worked at Zanatek wore a strict form of uniform.

"So what's going on?" he asked. "Why have you called us here at this unearthly hour?"

"We've run into a bit of a snag, I'm afraid," replied Xenides. "Apparently the testing we have been doing over the last few years has resulted in serious climatic changes, and people are dying of some new disease. It's happened on Trixis, Vantara, and now, Iltium. If we don't contain it, it could spread to Zanthium. Plus of course, there was the deaths from the sparks of the missiles that struck these planets."

"Then we have to stop the testing!" exclaimed Osmond. "We can't be held responsible for the deaths of millions of beings, just to advance technology!" he added earnestly, donning his glasses to read the report Xenides had just handed to him.

"I'm afraid it's not as easy as that Bill. We can't reverse the effects of the cardium oxide that's resulted from the detonations. They're calling this disease Neuroplasmosis. It affects the whole central nervous system, and is terminal." Before Osmond could reply, the others began to file into the conference room.

Malcolm addressed the meeting. "I've just been telling Osmond here of the problem we have hit with the testing we've been doing here, and it seems the resultant emanations of cardium oxide have led to a condition called Neuroplasmosis. You'll see all the details in the report in front of you. Grab something to eat while you read. There's plenty for everyone." Xenides had made certain that everything was catered to everyone's individual tastes and preferences.

Paul Osarias was the next to react to this devastating news. "I can't believe this! Do you mean that we are literally wiping out the galaxy from carrying out these tests? We've got to do something!"

"Well, what would you suggest, Paul? Put out an all-planets bulletin to advertise our monumental mistake?" Xenides retorted sarcastically. "Or perhaps we could just send out an inter-holovision to the leaders of each race saying, "Oops, we've made a bit of a blunder. So sorry you are going to lose thousands of your people!"

"Being sarcastic doesn't solve anything," said Miranda Tullage in what Xenides thought was a 'sickeningly calming tone'. "We have to act responsibly here, and let these poor people know what they are in for, so that they can make the right decisions. What do you think, Alexis?"

Now Alexis Madrinone, was in complete agreement with Miranda Tullage, but didn't want Xenides to know that -not until he knew a lot more about what was actually happening on these other planets. He wanted to see for himself, not be told second-hand. He'd always had misgivings about testing these missiles in space, and had voiced his concerns at the very beginning, but had been shouted down by the others.

"Look, before we make any snap decisions, maybe we should send someone to these planets to get more of an idea of just what exactly is going on there."

"Great idea!" exclaimed Xenides. "I take it that you are volunteering to go," he added enthusiastically.

"When do you want me to leave?" asked Alexis. "I'll need to take someone else with me."

"Take Miranda," suggested Xenides. "She sounds like she could use the break. Bit of an adventure for you eh?"

"Consider us gone," Miranda retorted as she tossed her shoulder-length blonde hair from her slim shoulders. She left with Alex, and the others finished reading the report, as they drank their drinks and ate their food.

"Patronizing old coot!" she exclaimed as she and Alexis exited the building.

"Just ignore him Miranda. He's just trying to get a rise out of you, hoping you'll take the bait," Alexis said, laughing at her outburst but in complete agreement with her.

"I'm not going to give him the satisfaction," she sniffed. Realizing how silly she was to let Xenides' patronization of her affect her, she laughed, too. But then, accepting the serious nature of their task she said "Let's get going! I want to see what's going on Trixis, Vantara and Iltium. Maybe we can do something to stop this disease spreading further."

"Count me in," replied Alexis, walking quickly and companionably alongside her.

✄ ✄ ✄

"Now let's get back to the business at hand. What's your opinion on this?" Xenides asked his remaining colleagues.

"I agree with Paul..." Amara Seng said. "We can't just sit idly by and watch thousands of people die, just because we need to win the technology race here!" Amara Seng hailed from the planet Iltium, and was medium height and feline-like in appearance.

Zenda Wariff, also from Iltium nodded in agreement. "How can we possibly justify this horror? It's absolutely incomprehensible!"

"I'm in no way intending to do that!" retorted Xenides, becoming more and more annoyed by the rising hysteria, and the comments being made by his executives. "But you have to realize that sacrifices have to be made in order to reach our goal."

"Yes, but at the risk of so many lives? Many of us have relatives on these planets!" exclaimed Tularis Plau, "Nothing can be worth the loss of so many lives!" He said with a stilted accent. He and many of the other settled aliens still found it hard to speak Terrian (Earthspeak) without it sounding very formal. He hailed from Vantara and was eight feet tall with a greenish tinge to his skin.

Most of the aliens from other planets had eventually adapted really well to the atmosphere on Zanthium, mutating over time, as needed, to cope with what had seemed a strange climate to them at first. Some hadn't been able to make this metamorphosis however, and had unfortunately died out. Only the strongest and fittest had survived this exacting planet.

Takrannoc Shaad, another Vantarian added, "I too cannot justify the deaths of so many people, and sleep well in my bed at night. These technological advances were to be for the betterment of the people in this galaxy, not lead to their demise. What were we thinking of when we agreed to such a a monstrous proposal?" He stammered.

"We have to be honest and tell our leaders of this galaxy know what we have done, and the ramifications of our actions, before it is too late to implement any strategies to survive," voiced Paul Osarias.

"Agreed!" chipped in Bill Osmond, once again fiddling with his Zanatek badge.

"All right, All right!" Xenides agreed, mainly to get them all out of his office, so he could concentrate on what his next strategy would be. "Leave it with me. I will take the responsibility of trying to rectify this situation. You just get on with your duties here."

Once alone, he began to formulate a plan.

THREE

TRIXIS

When Wandana entered the modest little home where she had spent her younger days when not in school, Uuffi's wrapped his arms around his eldest daughter in an enthusiastic welcome. Her mother's warm greeting was not far behind, followed by embraces from the rest of her family. It felt good to be home, despite the bad news she was about to tell them.

"How are things here, Dad?" she asked, as she laughingly disentangled herself from yet another sibling's embrace. "I noticed, as the shuttle flew over the fields, that there were fewer crops than usual and the ones I saw were quite spoiled," her face showing concern.

The smile instantly evaporated from her father's tired weatherbeaten face. "Not good, I'm afraid," he replied to his daughter, who now was being offered a cup of green ardmonium tea and a plate of derudian noodles with mushrooms by her mother. Wandana was famished; she had not eaten much since she left Xenide's office the night before, as she had been so worried. Not wanting to miss anything that her father was saying, she refused the meal her mother was offering with a shake of her head and the words "Maybe later." Her mother looked at her, shaking her head, before making her way back into the kitchen to finish preparing the evening meal.

"The springs and summers have been so hot and the autumns and winters so cold this year, that we have hardly been able to harvest enough to feed ourselves, never mind sell in the market-square. We lost a few of our people this year. Remember Vandutu the oldest man in our village?"

"Yes?" replied Wandana, dreading what was to come next. Everybody loved Vandutu, the wisest man on the island.

"Well he died during the cold winter. He could not keep himself warm because wood is so scarce now. Others have died, too, from trying to eat last year's meager crop. It went rotten before we could even harvest it," he added.

"I'm so sorry Dad," replied Wandana sadly, as she gave her dear father a warm hug.

Then, bracing herself she began: "That's what I am here to tell you. I know why the crops have been going bad, and the weather is changing here. The testing that Zanatek had been carrying out, has polluted the atmosphere with a chemical called Cardium oxide. Then there are the deaths of all those people from the missile testing" she added sadly.

"Car- what?" Talanta asked, returning from the kitchen to join in with the serious conversation between her husband and daughter.

"Cardiom oxide," her daughter explained. "For some

reason it has contaminated… uh I mean affected everything around us. I don't understand everything," she confessed. "I just overheard the company directors talking one day after one of their meetings."

"Oh Wandana!" exclaimed her shocked father. "How could you be involved with people who would do such things?" As he shook his head in disapproval.

"Honestly, Dad, I didn't know. I have just found out about this myself, and I came here to tell you everything I know, in the hope that maybe you might know what to do. I know that I can't stay there anymore. But I also know that you and Mum need the money that I send to keep things going here," she said sadly, staring into the ardmonium tea, her mother had handed her, as if she would find an answer there.

"Of course you can't work there!" exclaimed her mother vehemently. "Don't worry about us, we can survive. We have always survived, have we not Uuffi?"

"Yes," replied her father. "Now eat something my child. You can't think properly on an empty stomach, and after our meal, I will call the elders together, and maybe we can decide between us what needs to be done to survive yet another crisis."

FOUR

TO TRIXIS

Miranda Tullage and Alexis Madrione were travelling on the same shuttle as Wandana, however they were too caught up in their own agendas to notice other passengers.

"Well, what you make of what we heard in there, Lexi?" asked Miranda, as she tucked into the delicious but wholesome Balantan meal that had been placed in front of her, by one of the shuttle attendants.

"I feel the same way you do, Randa," he replied to his old friend. "The sacrifice of thousands of people just to further Zanatek's selfish objectives is unthinkable." I'm just glad that we've been given this opportunity to go and investigate just exactly what has been occurring on Trixis."

"Me too," she replied. "I'm glad you feel the same way I

do about all this," she added, as she passed him the lubruckan sauce for his equally delicious Ganganeen rice dish. "Many of Malcolm's decisions have annoyed me in the past, but this is just plain insanity!" she exclaimed.

"The sooner we get there, the better I'll like it," he replied. "I just hope we're not too late to do anything!"

✂ ✂ ✂

Miranda and Alexis had met when Miranda had first joined Zanatek,.They were single and enjoyed each other's company. They had quickly become good friends, and that friendship eventually led to something more intimate. However it hadn't worked out for them. "Too many differences," Miranda had told her close friends, Zenda Wariff and Amara Seng.

"She's just too stubborn and opinionated," Alexis had told his good friends Takranoc Shaad and Tularis Plau.

Their break up was a mutual decision and, after a period of adjustment, they were able to resume their friendship.

Now here they were travelling to Trixis together, Miranda mused, as they had once planned to do for a "great holiday," Alexis had said, before he had been transferred to another branch of Zanatek, on a different planet for a whole year!

Miranda was brought out of her reverie, by the sound of Alexis' voice announcing that they had arrived on Trixis, and "We had better get organized if we want to get off the shuttle quickly".

FIVE

THE GATHERING

Uuffi gathered the elders together. Wandana never ceased to be amazed at the love and respect he could command from these wise old people, and she felt much honored at being allowed to attend this gathering of such venerated men and women.

"Welcome, my friends!" Uuffi said solemly. He usually enjoyed these meetings with these men and women who had experienced so much of life on and off Trixis, and never tired of hearing of their adventures when they were younger. But today was a different story. Until now, his daughter had been too young to take part in such assemblies, but now it was her time to tell the elders what was happening throughout the galaxy, and why the climate on Trixis had changed so erratically, and why so many people were becoming so ill.

"Don't be afraid to tell them everything," Uuffi encouraged her. "The more they know, the more power they will have to deal with this terrible situation".

"We have serious business to discuss. My daughter Wandana has come all the way from Zanthium to seek our help about the galaxy crisis."

The villagers listened, as Wandana took a deep breath and began.

"As you may know I work for Zanatek. For many years now, Zanatek has been experimenting with missiles and has fired many into our atmosphere." She began tentatively. "From these missiles a toxic gas called Cardium oxide has been excreted which has resulted in contamination of the ground in which we grow our vegetables and fruits, and the lakes and rivers on our planet to be contaminated. This contamination is causing crops to ripen too quickly and become spoiled. It is poisoning the fish, and has produced a disease in our people and the animals, that affects the central nervous system and the brain. This disease is called Neuroplasmosis, and, if not treated effectively, results in death. Already thousands of people from neighbouring planets have been lost, when the debris hit these planets."

She paused, waiting for the gravity of what she was saying to sink in.

Tuwub Suud spoke first. "Did you know about all this when you went to work for Zanatek? "He asked suspiciously.

"No," replied Wandana. "I just happened to overhear a conversation between the Managing Director, – Malcolm Xenides and a couple of his associates," she added vehemently. "He thinks I am too young to understand what is going on. But I understand very well."

"Well at least that is something!" exclaimed Tanaka Ulosis. Very relieved to know that the young woman was not involved in the conspiracy. Tanaka had been quite involved in Wandana's moral education, and would have been very disappointed to hear that her pupil had strayed so far from the path.

Benetin Puut spoke next: "Which other planets have been affected?"

"Many planets have been affected," replied Wandana sadly. "Vantara and Iltium are two that like us, have lost a lot of their people."

"Then we must do all that we can to prevent it spreading any further," stated Benetin Puut.

"But what can we do? We know so little about this disease?" asked Shalaad Watami, sadly shaking her head, and who until then had been listening, trying to take everything in.

"We must learn all that we can about this disease," replied Uuffi. "The more that we can learn, the more of a chance we have of finding a cure or stopping it from spreading further." He smiled confidently at his daughter; she smiled back, but not as confidently. She did not have a clue as to how she was going to go about this. It would undoubtedly involve spying on Xenides to get further information, so that she, her people and others on the affected planets, could fight this disease.

"What are the symptoms of this disease?" asked Shalaad Watami.

"We know that it affects the central nervous system and is terminal, unless the scientists can find a cure." replied Wandana. She waited for the assembly to take this all in before continuing, but was interrupted by Benetin Putt who wanted to know; "Is it contagious?"

"The scientists don't seem to think so," said Wandana. "It attacks the brain, and has symptoms similar to the disease multiple sclerosis that existed on Terra in the twentieth century. This disease causes gradual brain and muscular degeneration.

However it is not believed to be spread through contact with other people who have contracted this disease. There is no infectious rash involved, or anything like that," she added.

"Well at least that is something," someone murmured.

"I know I'm not being very helpful," said Wandana, "but this is all I know at the moment." She had never felt more helpless in her life.

"You cannot know that that you do not know," said Tanaka Tulosis. "She is not a scientist everyone. We must be patient and wait for them to find a cure. In the meantime we must not eat this seasons' crops or fish in our oceans. Maybe that way we can keep ourselves safe from this awful disease."

"But how will we survive? We have only enough uncontaminated crops to last this season. What will we eat after then?" asked Shalaad Watami.

"I'm afraid I do not know" replied Tanka Tulosis. "Hopefully the scientists will have found a cure before we run out of food to feed our people."

And so the meeting ended, and although they left with rather heavy hearts, they also left with a glimmer of hope, that the learned scientists could find a way to fight this disease that was blighting their lives.

✻ ✻ ✻

Xenides lost no time in getting in touch with the people that could help him deal with this annoying situation.

"Yes," he began as he reached the person with whom he wished to speak. "Whatever it takes, and however much it costs. Money is no object. I want this situation rectified as soon as possible. Do you hear me?"

"Coming through loud and clear," replied Zeniden Quossack quietly. Who was an old hand at rectifying annoying problems. "How many do you want me to take out?" he asked calmly, coldly.

"Quite a few, I'm afraid. It's regrettable, but necessary if I want to succeed in this operation."

"Consider the situation rectified," replied Zeniden and hung up before Xenides could say any more.

Quossack was a man of few words, but very effective in the execution of his duties.

This was not the first time that Xenides had made use of Quossack's exacting expertise, when people had got in the way of this objectives. But his conscience did twinge a bit in this instance. After all he had known these people at Zanatek for about ten years now, and had become rather attached to them.

Still, it had to be done. Nothing could get in the way of his objective. Nothing must get in the way of Xenide's plan for Zanatek's expansion into the galaxy, and his subsequent mining of Relium, which would put the planet of Zantium way ahead in technology.

🟆 🟆 🟆

Miranda and Alexis were now fighting their way through customs. There had been quite a few random attacks from the extremist group Tajmalhut, who blamed the "decadent Mandacar" for the erratic changes in climate all over the galaxy, and had been responsible for the many terrorist attacks that had been occurring all over the galaxy, and were becoming bolder every time they succeeded. Unlike the Wandaggi, who advocated a more peaceful way of dealing with the situation.

Rioting in the streets by the beings affected with Neuroplasmosis had also occurred on the planets, along with those protesting against the firing of the missiles in the first place. These had been quickly and expertly quelled by the authorities on each of the planets however. Besides many of the planets' inhabitants had been too sick to start riots anyway.

Eventually Miranda and Alexis made their way to the exit. Every item of their luggage had been searched, and they had been asked why they were on Trixis. They had both replied "To visit a friend," - as Miranda knew that Wandana the young personal assistant lived somewhere on this planet. Alexis remembered hearing that she lived on the South side of this once beautiful island planet.

Although travel had been restricted somewhat as there were fears that the Neuroplasmosic disease might be contagious, Alexis and Miranda had been given special dispensation, arranged by Xenides. It certainly paid to have high people in high places at this tense time.

And so they set off in search of Wandana, hoping she could fill them in about what had been happening here on Trixis.

❋　❋　❋

Paul Osarias was sitting watching television when a knock came at the door.

"I'll get it, honey. You've had a hard day," he called over his shoulder. "Bill said he might call over to talk about a couple of things." It was the last thing he would ever say. His wife Brenda screamed as her husband slumped to the floor, his body then promptly disintegrated.

People came running out of their pods, (apartments), but it was too late. Only ashes and bone were found. Both had been incinerated. On the floor of their luxury pod, no-one saw Zeniden Quossack press his state of the art holowatch which transported him out of the dead couple's pod, and into the street far below.

SIX

INTRODUCTIONS

Alexis and Miranda finally arrived at the hotel where they had booked to stay a few days. They went to their rooms to freshen up before meeting in the hotel bar.

"How well do you know Wandana?" Alexis asked Miranda, as they sipped on their cool 'Island Special' drinks.

"Not very well," Miranda replied, stirring her drink with her cocktail stick.

"I know that she's Xenide's personal assistant, and that she has been at Zanatek for about three years, and that she grew up on this planet. But that's all."

"We should leave about eight tomorrow morning," he said. "I'm not sure how long it will take to get there. God knows how reliable the transport is at the moment with all that has been happening!" He said, running his fingers through his short cropped brown hair with frustration.

"Good idea," she replied. But they stayed on, talking well into the night.

They had already acquired a map of the South-side of the island planet before they had been transported from the holoport to the shuttle, so all that was left to do, next day, was set off for the dock where they found themselves on board a rickety old form of transport that took them on a meandering tour for about four hours, until at last they spotted what looked like Wandana's village.

They arrived just about lunch-time.

⌘ ⌘ ⌘

"It's done," Quossack informed Xenides on the holotext . "One less annoyance to get in your way."

"Any problems?" asked Xenides.

"No," Quossack replied in an emotionless voice. "Everything went without a hitch. I was in and out, without anyone even being aware I was there." He congratulated himself.

"Good," Xenides replied as he lit himself a cigar. "We don't want any more complications."

"Glad to be of service," Quossack replied. "Let me know when you want the next annoyance taken care of."

"I will. Stay out of sight till you hear from me. You hear?"

"Coming through loud and clear," replied Quossack, then hung up.

Xenides was alone with his own thoughts. 'It couldn't be helped,' he said to himself. 'They were in the way. Nothing can get in the way of my plans for Zanatek.'

He poured himself a stiff drink, and settled into his luxurious black leather armchair.

⁂

Wandana was busily engaged in conversation with her brothers and sisters when there came a knock at the door.

She opened it and was confronted with two colleagues from her workplace. 'I wonder what they are doing here?' she thought as she invited them in, and introduced them to her family.

In all the time she had been at Zanatek, these two people had only spoken to her for a few minutes.

"Welcome to our home!" Uuffi said, happy to have more visitors.

Miranda and Alexis followed Wandana into the kitchen where she was helping her mother with the noon-time meal.

"How did you know where I lived?" Wandana asked a little shyly.

She had always looked up to Miranda, considering her to be a good role model. Miranda was self-assured, confident yet still very feminine, everything that Wandana wanted to be, and knew what she wanted from life, whereas Wandana was still finding her way.

Alex had an easy-going quality about him. "You weren't hard to find once we had the map to this area," he said with an easy smile.

"Miranda smiled too, but remembering the seriousness of the situation, she began to explain why they were there.

"How much do you understand about what has been happening here in Trixis?" she asked Wandana.

"Enough to know that it is Zanatek and their infernal

testing that is causing the climate changes here and on Vantara and Iltium, and the deaths of so many people."

"Not to mention many other planets," added Alexis, as he reluctantly dragged his gaze away from the delicious food that was being prepared. He felt guilty for thinking of satisfying his hunger when he should be concentrating on more important issues.

Talanta offered them something to keep them going until lunch was ready, when she had led them to the room reserved for special occasions.

Miranda and Alexis tried not to be too hasty eating, but they hadn't eaten since they had boarded the outmoded form of transport that had brought them to Uuffi and Talanta's home.

"Yes," Uuffi said. "We have lost many good crops the last few seasons, not to mention the fish in our lakes and rivers. And many of our people and animals who have eaten these contaminated crops and fish have died."

"Yes. A lot of people on other planets have died because of Cardium oxide poisoning," added Miranda. "I was so sorry to hear about your people too, Uuffi." she said compassionately.

"Yes, it has been a terrible year, and it is going to get worse isn't it?" he asked.

"I'm afraid so," replied Alexis. "Unless we can find a way to counteract the effects of the cardium oxide, many more will die from neuorplasmosis."

"Then we must find a way to do that," said Wandana's father with conviction.

"Xenides is crazy to think he's going to get away with missile testing now!" Wandana exclaimed. "There must be other people besides us who are against what he is doing. The risks he is taking with the lives of everyone in this galaxy."

"Of course there are," replied Miranda. "But they are too frightened to speak up, for fear of losing their jobs."

"Their lives, maybe?" added Alexis.

"What do you mean?" asked Miranda.

"Well Xenides didn't get to where he is by being a mister nice guy, 'Randa."

"Well, yes I know that, Lexi. But just how far do you think he is prepared to go?"

"Let's hope we don't have to find out!" replied Alexis earnestly.

Then leading them into the main room, Uuffi said, "Let's eat! We must not waste such a delicious meal that my beautiful wife has cooked," and he put his arm tenderly around Talanta's ample waist.

Neither Miranda nor Alexis knew that this food was the last of the Galantez's good crop, and that they might not eat as well again, for a long time.

Talanta laughed and playfully pushed Uuffi away. "Behave yourself, old man. We have company."

Everybody laughed, and for a while at least, the mood became a little lighter, as they all tucked into the meal on their plates.

❄ ❄ ❄

It didn't take long for the news of the murders of Paul and Brenda Osarias to spread throughout the employees of Zanatek. After all he had been one of the company's top notch men, and both he and his wife had been very much loved by all the employees. Equally the other residents who lived in their pod block could not believe that 'such a nice couple,' had died in such a violent way. After all, their neighborhood was a quiet 'civilized place' to live, where nothing out of the ordinary ever happened, especially not "dear neighbors being incinerated in their own living-rooms! " exclaimed Elthia Multar, who had lived there forty years. "The police are going to have a full-time job solving this one," Petrov Walanski who had lived there almost as long as Elthia Multar had added.

Meanwhile Malcolm Xenides said all the right things at all the right times, answering Chief Inspector Gerdanian Athos' questions and attending Paul and Brenda's memorial service, all the while congratulating himself at having eliminated a real 'pain in the ass!' when he finally had a moment to himself. But more lives would need to be sacrificed in order to protect the corporation that he had spent his own sweat and blood setting up. It was going to be a messy business, but how else was he to get the people he really wanted up there with him? The ones that supported him and his ideals without question?

Unfortunately he was going to have to wait until all the fuss died down before he could even think of contacting Quossack again to arrange the next termination.

It was late in the night and Miranda and Alexis announced that it was time to leave so the Galantez family could get some sleep. But they insisted that the visitors stay the night, as it was "such as long way back to your hotel," Talanta had insisted as she Wandana and her younger sister Weilana helped to organize somewhere for them to bed down for the night. Miranda was to sleep in the girls' room, and Alexis was to bunk in with the boys.

Wandana wasted no time before talking to Miranda about what had been going on at Zanatek. "I just can't believe that Malcolm Xenides is responsible for so many deaths. It's just unthinkable!"

"He fooled all of us for a long time," replied Miranda, "but no more! He has to take responsibility for what he has done. But we are going to need all the proof we can get. As his P.A. you must have a lot of access to his files etc. Would you be willing to gather evidence so we can nail this bastard?" asked Miranda.

"Yes, of course," replied Wandana. "I was hoping you'd ask me. I was planning to do it myself, but it's better to have others to back me up."

"Good for you! I knew you had guts," Miranda whispered so as not to waken the other girls.

"But you've only spoken to me a few times! How could you tell just from a couple of conversations?"

"You don't get as far as I have without learning a few things about people. I could see that you had what it takes to help us," replied Miranda with admiration in her voice. "Now all we have to do is let Lexi know that you're working with us," she said, yawning. "But we'll leave it till tomorrow. I'm dog tired now. Sleep well, we're going to be very busy tomorrow."

"Goodnight," said Wandana, wondering where she was going to get the courage that her mentor believed she had, to spy on her boss. But she was determined not to let Miranda and Alexi down.

SEVEN

BACK TO ZANATEK

Amara Seng and Zenda Wariff hadn't heard from Miranda for nearly a week and were becoming worried about both her and Alexis. Tularis Plau and Takrannoc Shadd were just as worried about them, but didn't want to alarm the girls by showing their concern.

After the tragic deaths of Paul and Brenda Osarias, Zanatek was not the same. Gone was the employees' trust and faith in what the company was doing, which was replaced by horror and disbelief that Zanatek's executives had been complicit in the annihilation of thousands of beings. If only they had been told the truth; given the facts. And if these innocent beings going about their daily lives could be obliterated in what seemed to be a blink of an eye, and if such good people like the Osarias' so violently, what might happen to them if they didn't agree with Xenides and his unscrupulous policies?

"I hope Randa and Lexi are ok," Amara whispered to Zenda as they were pouring yet again over the report that Xenides had given them. Their brains were racing from all the coffee they had been drinking, but they tried remain calm as they re-read the statistics.

"Don't worry, I'm sure they are ok. They are good at looking after each other," replied Zenda, even though she herself had grave fears; for Miranda and Alexis had not had enough time to tell them exactly where they were going, having left quite hurriedly.

Tularis and Takrannoc were engaged in the same procedure.

"It doesn't matter how many times we go over this report. Nothing can change the fact that thousands of beings have died because of what we have been involved in," Takrannoc finally announced to them all.

The group decided to all meet at Takrannoc's pod, as it was not too far from the lab. "Hopefully you weren't followed," he had said as he had led them into his tastefully decorated but modest pod. All the employees of Zanatek lived in fully-furnished pod blocks, financed by Zanatek. They were allowed to choose the furnishings themselves however, and Takrannoc had chosen very well. He had only to press his holowatch for everything in his apartment to operate – lights, pod cleaner, food creator, etc. All the mod cons you could thing of were operated by his holowatch.

"How did we ever allow ourselves to be so taken in?" exclaimed Tularis vehemently. "Why didn't we ask more questions? Why did we trust such an unscrupulous man?"

"Don't feel so guilty. We were all taken in," replied Amara. We wanted to believe in what we were doing. I know it was naïve, but we all thought that we were helping to achieve technological advances which would be good for the universe."

"Yes," Zenda added. "But we didn't take into account that not everyone in this universe has an altruistic agenda. We were blinded by the materialistic trappings that came with working for a man like Xenides. We wanted to feel positive about the work we were doing at Zanatek, so we allowed ourselves to be lulled into a false sense of security. That is something we can't deny," she concluded, feeling just as exasperated and guilt- ridden as her colleagues.

"So what do we do now? We have to get the message out to the public about what has been going on here. I hope to Gabba, Randa and Lexi are ok!"

"You're right, Tularis," replied Takranoc. And he proceeded to holotext Alexi and Miranda one more time, hoping that this time he could get through, but again neither answered.

"It's getting late, guys. Maybe we should be getting back to our homes. Besides we all have to be alert and on our toes if we are going to beat Xenides at his own game. He's a dangerous and wily man, who it seems will stop at nothing to get where he wants to be," stated Tularis as he escorted Amara and Zenda out, and safely to their pod, which they shared.

The following day, Alexis, Miranda, and Wandana made their farewells to the Galantez family, hugging them warmly, and fervently promising to be back as soon as they could. Father and daughter embraced one more time, but were too overcome with emotion to say how much they would miss and would worry about each other.

Wandana had a difficult path before her, and would have to summon up all her courage to do what was expected of her. Her father and the villagers would need to find out everything they could about Neuroplasmosis. Hopefully some of the younger remaining islanders would be able to be schooled in this, if they could find the scientists to teach them. They and the whole village would now be travelling unchartered waters. But although filled with great trepidation, they would follow the father and daughter's lead, and their new friends Alexis and Miranda – and do anything so that they, their children and their children's children would survive this devastating disease.

✄ ✄ ✄

Back on the shuttle, Miranda wasted no time in contacting Takrannoc and the rest of their friends. She let him know that indeed she, Alexi and Wandana were safe, well, and on their way back to her pod. "Would you meet us there?" "It's not all good news I'm afraid," Miranda added. Takrannoc, was overjoyed that his dear friends were safe, and said he would let the others know, and that he was sure they would all agree to go to Miranda's pod.

Takrannoc, Tularis, Amara and Zenda were a bit surprised when Wandana entered the room with them, but were too polite to ply them with questions. They had been friends long enough to know that all would be revealed in due course.

"We were visiting Wandana's family on Trixis" Alexis volunteered, smiling at Wandana warmly.

When they were all seated comfortably with drinks in front of them, Miranda said, "We had never been made to feel so welcome by people we had never met before," added Miranda. "It was lovely to meet them and spend time with them, even though it wasn't under happy circumstances," she added ruefully. "Let's eat before we get down to business."

They enjoyed the hastily prepared dishes by Miranda. Alex was greatly surprised as he didn't even know she could cook.

'Something else she has kept from me,' he mused to himself. 'Maybe we should have worked harder at our relationship." He tucked into the healthy yet succulent meal that was before him. He looked across the table at Miranda, who just looked at him, giving the enigmatic smile that he had always found delightfully inscrutable.

"Right let's get serious" he said, tearing his eyes away from such a lovely distraction. He and Miranda quickly described the situation they had found on Trixis, with Wandana interjecting a few times to explain what she had found out about Xenides. Then Takrannoc explained all that had transpired at his pod and how Paul and Brenda Osarias had been murdered.

Miranda, Alexis and Wandana were shocked and saddened to hear of their deaths.

"Whatever you do, don't let Xenides know that we're back!" exclaimed Miranda.

"No, we need to keep an element of surprise," Alexis added.

Amara and Zenda were a bit put out with such an obvious request. "Of course we won't let on that you are back. "Do you think we are stupid?"

"No, no. That's not what we meant," interjected Randa, always the mediator and diplomat in such delicate situations. 'Just managed to make an absolute ass of myself in front of Lexi. You think I would be past that by now,' she upbraided herself. She handed out the drinks and exotic deserts that Amara and Zelda had brought with them. "I just meant that if Xenides would have such a nice couple as Paul and Brenda killed, as we think he has, who else would he be willing to kill? Just how many deaths has he actually been responsible for?"

"Wandana has agreed to do a bit of snooping for us," announced Alexis, trying to lighten the situation a bit, smiling at Wandana with admiration. "She is his P.A., so she can probably get her hands on some pretty incriminating stuff, which we or even the Board don't have access to."

Everyone agreed that it was a good plan, as long as Wandana felt comfortable enough about doing it. It could after all be very dangerous for her operation.

Takrannoc wasn't sure that she was actually up to the task. 'She's a bit young,' the Vantarian thought to himself. But being of a reflective nature, he decided to keep his doubts to himself. After all he may be wrong. He hoped this was the case.

'Tomorrow is going to be a strange day,' Wandana was thinking. 'I will have to still be supportive of Xenides, even though I now hate him with a fervour. Mustn't let my feelings interfere with what I have to do.' She forced herself to concentrate on the conversation going on around her.

Everyone in the room, although appearing light-hearted, bantering with each other good-naturedly as they ate, were fully aware of the gravity of the situation. They couldn't turn back now. They had come too far. Xenides' crazy quest for power had to be stopped. But how? And who else was a part of this, and who else had given him the support to get as far as he had in Zanatek? These were other questions that had to be answered.

"It's probably time we started making tracks," suggested Tularis. "Randa, Lexi and Wandana must be pretty done in after all their travelling."

"Yes," agreed Zenda. "We should probably let you three get your rest."

"Safe journey," they said quietly. And then they were gone.

No-one was tactless enough to ask if Alexi was leaving with them, or staying behind with Miranda. They had all known each other for long enough to know not to do that.

Although they were really dying to know how things were going with them after their adventures.

Miranda and Alexis began clearing away the remnants of the little feast, and then Miranda pressed her holowatch and the dishes in the dish-cleaning machine were cleaned in no time. Then they dashed off to change out of their corporate uniforms into some old, serviceable clothes, so that they would not be conspicuous where they were going to be hiding out.

"I think Wandana has a bit of a crush on you Lex," Miranda said playfully when they were sure that Miranda was out of earshot.

"Yes, I know," he replied. "But she's too young for me," he said.

"Let her down easily, won't you," she advised him good-naturedly but seriously.

"Don't worry," he whispered. "Wouldn't want to put her off men forever." With a cheeky grin that at one time 'Randa would not have been able to resist. "But I know what you mean."

"Well that didn't happen when you and I split up," she quipped back

"That's good to know," he replied playfully, but seriously as well. He'd always felt bad that they hadn't been able to work things out. 'Still who knows with all the time we'll be spending together, maybe…Ah, come to your senses man and concentrate on the job at hand,' he rebuked himself.

They had already discussed with their friends where they would be going, so that they could keep in touch with each other whenever it was possible. Wandana was to stay here at Miranda's place, as it was nearer for her to get to Zanatek.

With that all organized, they settled down for the night. Wandana and Miranda were in the bedroom, with Wandana on a roll out mattress and blankets. Alexis was on the comfortable complimentary couch, with a blanket, given to him by Miranda. "Thanks hon," he said before he could stop himself. As he took the blanket offered to him. It was hard to tell who blushed the most as old memories came to the surface.

"Yes, well, sleep well," Miranda murmured, and left the room. She wasn't sure what she was feeling. And she wasn't sure if she was ready to find out just yet, as she made her way back to her room.

"Yeah, you too," murmured Alexis. 'I guess it is still going to take a while for us to completely forget what we were to each other,' he thought to himself, as he snuggled down into the couch for a few hours sleep before they would have to leave the next day. He hugged his pillow like he would never let it go, not that he was aware of that however.

"So what's between you and Alexis?" asked Wandana mischievously.

"Lexi? Oh nothing. We did have something going a few years ago, but it didn't work out. We're just good friends now," she added, hoping that the warmth in her cheeks didn't show.

Wandana was about to ask more, but Miranda cut her short. "We really need to get some sleep now, as we are all going to be very busy tomorrow. Night Wandana. Sleep well". Miranda snuggled down thankfully into the protection of her doona.

�֎ ✖ ✖

On their way home, Takrannoc, Tularis, Zena and Amara were full of questions. "Who might be next on Xenides' hit list?" "If he could so easily kill two of the most loved and respected members of the board, how were Takrannoc and Co. going to protect themselves from the same fate? One thing for sure," stated Takrannoc. "None of us at Zanatek is safe there anymore. All the luxury in the world does not make up for the fact that we have been involved in something that has put all of us in danger because we have dared to disagree with his practices."

"I worry for Wandana, too," added Amara. "She is still very young, and impressionable."

"I think she will do fine," interjected Tularis. "She had the sense to trust Lexi and Randa with what she knew of the goings on at Zanatek. I think they know what they are doing, suggesting her for this operation."

"Yes," added Zenda. "Wandana has a good, sensible head on her shoulders, and genuinely wants to help her people. You can't ask for much more than that."

They all agreed they should all stay at his place, for the next few days, instead of going home to their own pods. Takrannoc was pretty sure that they were being watched now. His pod was large enough to accomodate them, also he suggested that he had the best form of security that money could buy. It would be safer if they stayed together, and they could be found easily when needed.

In the meantime, Takrannoc was going to send an urgent message, to his old war buddy Vandarken Washawski to let him know that he, Takrannoc, and five others would need a place to hole up away from Xenides and his henchmen.

EIGHT

CHIEF INSPECTOR
ATHOS GRENADARIAN

Wandana dutifully but nervously returned to work. Telling her
colleagues just enough about her visit to see her parents to ensure
that Xenides did not become suspicious, and carefully omitting
any mention of spending time there with Alexis and Miranda.

Xenides asked all the right questions to make himself
sound as caring, and then promptly dismissed any thought
of her. He had more important things to do, than waste time
talking to this girl about her family, even if her family, or in
fact their whole island planet, was in danger of extinction.
"Glad to have you back," he said. "Haven't been able to find
a single thing around here. Everything has gone to the dogs
with the investigation and everything."

This was just what the young P. A. wanted, to be indispensable yet inconspicuous and to blend in with the rest of the Zanatek employees, just as Miranda and Alexis had advised her to do.

When an opportunity eventually presented itself, she was more excited, and a little more nervous, than she thought she would be. After all it was a great risk she was taking.

Eventually, the talk about the murders of the Zanatek employees began to die down. Chief Inspector Athos Grenadarian, however, had not given up the investigation. He knew that when dealing with such a mastermind like Xenides, he was going to have to tread very carefully. He was fairly certain that the CEO had not just had this couple disposed of, but quite a long list of others who had got in his way. Athos had had his eye on Xenides for quite a few years now, but the wily old man had been leading him a merry dance. "Just couldn't make the charges stick," Athos complained gruffly to Wallach Rennik, his second-in-charge. "This time though, would be different, Athos told himself. This, time, I'm going to get him!" There was a hit man involved. He was sure of it.

"I'm damned sure he did it!" he exclaimed to Rennik, who was in the process of going through all the data that they had of such "low lives", as Athos had put it. "And I'm damned sure he had a lot of help too," he added with conviction. He was on his twelfth cup of coffee for the day, so his brain was racing a mile a minute.

Rennik had cut out the coffee after his fifth cup, and was now drinking lots of water to prevent dehydration. He was trying to get Athos to do the same, but with little result. Athos had already had one massive heart attack, and to Rennik it looked like he was happily on the way to another.

"Ok, so we know he has a lot of questionable connections with questionable beings," Athos began, helping himself to yet another cup of coffee, despite the disapproving look from Rennik.

"And we know he has the means to hire the best hit man/men in the business," added Rennik.

"Right," said Athos, helping himself to yet another cup of coffee, despite the disapproving look from Rennik.

"So where all his money come from?" Ignoring that look, Athos asked, "I don't just mean the money he's made in his business ventures. I mean all the little incidentals that, on their own, mean nothing, but when all lumped together...makes a very interesting macabre picture," finished Rennik.

"Well, yeah" added Athos, who was beginning to value his chief detective a lot more than he had in the past. He'd certainly been doing his homework, he thought approvingly.

At first he had rather resented being forced to take Rennik under his wing, after his former partner and best friend, Barnus Onedin, a Raksian from Raksia, who had been his best-man at Athos' wedding, had been killed in the line of duty, defending Rennik. Rennik at young rookie at the time had tried to foil a break in at the local grocery shop, without calling for back-up.

It had taken a long time for Athos to get over Barnus' death, and to forgive Rennik, for his impetuosity, or as Athos had put at the time for his "damned foolhardiness" However due mostly to Rennik's patience and easy-going nature, Athos had come to realize that what had happened to Barnus was not a one-off thing, as it was part of being in police business of protecting the innocent and vulnerable. So the initial wariness with each other had become a comfortable friendship, and Athos, now a widower, would often have dinner with Rennik and his wife. In fact he was pretty much a part of Rennik's family.

"Look, we've been at this for hours," said Rennik,

bringing Athos out of his reverie. "Let's go and grab a proper meal at my place. It'll help us to think better." The young detective could see that his friend was very tired, and in need of a good solid meal. "I'll just call Tulei, and let her know we're on our way."

Even though Tulei had had a very hectic day at the hospital, the busy registrar said she would be happy to feed Athos yet again. She was just as concerned for his welfare as Rennik, and didn't want him to be rushed to the hospital, and have paddles applied, only to lose him, as had happened today, with a patient about the same age.

Athos was more than happy to comply. He really enjoyed the young couple's company, and realized just how much he needed to get away from the office and unwind a bit. He'd still be thinking about the case of course, but at least he'd be in a more conducive environment, and more able to look at this situation from a different angle.

NINE

THE BASARIAN RESISTANCE

Vandarken Washawski, Leader of the Basarian resistance, was waiting impatiently with furrowed brow, as he poured over his plans, to hear from his friends Takrannoc Shaad and Tularis Plau.

The last that he had heard, was that they had successfully escaped the clutches of Xenides, and were staying at Takrannoc's high-security apartment. The plan was that they were to meet him at Washawski's compound when it was safe to travel, by night. Hopefully, Xenides did not find them in the meantime.

Washawski had seen it all…

Having survived the Rantulian second occupation, back in 7893, and escaped the horrific death camps – 800,000 having been exterminated by Rantulians, he went on to join the allies' space programme, becoming part of the now famous and highly-decorated Squadron 802, then the Basarian Water Rats, equally courageous and highly decorated.

For many years, Vandarken and his dear comrades in-arms, men and women, had struggled fearlessly and tirelessly to free both his and other planets, initially from Rantulia, and their insanely driven Vexer Rantin, and then from other dictators.

Finally, the Rantulian invasion was stopped, and the Rantulians surrendered. Then was the time to begin to heal...

Many years had gone by, and although Vandarken had tried hard to forget the devastating past, it was a long time before he could look at a blue- faced, blue-eyed Rantulian, without feeling a desire to "take-him out". This he had explained to his daughter, who had listened in shock and anger, was his reason for him not wishing for her to go out with the Rantulians of her generation. .... But that attitude too, changed with time, and now, many inhabitants of the different planets, were interspecies.

Although he was very worried about Takrannoc and Tulais, he was also looking forward to working with his older friends again from the war. He had to admit that he excitement of that period he sometimes missed.

Hopefully he would hear from Takrannoc and Tularis soon. He had aleady sent out some of his people to see if they were in sight yet.

Many Basarians had been saved from extermination by the very courageous, Ranski Verker of Talden Industries, who had employed and helped them to escape. But despite the rescued Basarians' gratitude, Ranski continued to believe that he hadn't done enough, and could have in fact done a great deal more.

Two other men that Washawski had also equally respected were Tarquin Vorinski and Bartau Lauser, who had also escaped the death camps and had written a huge expose of all the atrocities committed there against Basarians, Iltians, Vantarans and many other dwellers of Galaxies.

And now Vandarken was needed again…

✂ ✂ ✂

The opportunity for Wandana to help her friends came around a lot sooner than she could have ever imagined. Xenides had gone out on what he had referred to as "a little business trip", and had left her in charge of all the office.

She had quickly busied herself in securing the public and confidential information she needed in relation to the Neuroplasmosis Case, and had copied the material onto the CMD (Cerebral Memory Disc) that had been painlessly attached to the back of her skull, when she had commenced working for Zanatek. Only the Personal Assistants were fitted with these, which made them walking efficient filing systems.

She had been extremely nervous, that she might be discovered. But it seemed that all the staff had been more concerned with their own affairs, to bother about what an immigrant was doing.

Later in the safety of Takrannoc's pod, she transferred the much-needed information onto the holovision for everyone to see. Everything they needed to know was there – dates, cases, and number of deaths.

They were all shocked by the number of terminal cases, 4,889,214 listed. Miranda and the others were very impressed with what she had shown them, but were equally distressed at the number of terminal cases, which was still climbing.

"We must get this info to Athos a.s.a.p.," said Takrannoc.

TEN

HEADQUARTERS

The next day found Takrannoc and his followers onboard a shuttle bound for Delosa, and then finally to police headquarters, where the CMD information and the other material Randa and Alexi had obtained was painlessly extracted from Wandana's head, and put in front of him on the holovision device.

Athos had grabbed Takrannoc in an affectionate bear-hug, which was returned with gusto. "How are you old devil?" asked Takrannoc to Athos, who responded with, "What have you been up to now Shaad?"

Takrannoc quickly filled him in with all the details. Explaining how Wandana had transferred the incriminating data onto her CMD, which was now in front of him.

"Right now, down to the business at hand," he said, after they had viewed the information. "I know someone who will be extremely interested to hear and see all this evidence. This is enough to put that old bastard away for the rest of his life. Now we need to get you people to safety, and somewhere where Xenides can't find you. In the meantime go back to Takrannoc's pod," as he escorted them out of his office.

Rennik was to fly with them, as a security measure.

�֍ ✖ ✖

When Miranda, Alex and friends arrived back at Takrannoc's pod, a nasty surprise awaited them. It had been ransacked. Furniture, books and papers were strewn everywhere, and the holovision machine was destroyed. Takrannoc decided they should go to Warshawski's compound on their own and not wait for Athos.

"It is no longer safe to be here," he said, "We must go!"

In their haste to leave they neglected to let Athos know of their plans.

ELEVEN

THE B.C.P

Athos wasted no time in getting touch with Pander Tran, Head of the B.CP. (The Bureau of Crime Prevention), and they arranged that they should meet in the nearby Reserve Park, to discuss the procedure needed to get Takrannoc and his friends safely to Washawski, (also an old comrade-in arms also to Athos).

Having already met with Takrannoc, Plau, Tullage, Seng and Midrione, he had been very impressed with them especially the girls, and their willingness to work with him. He greatly respected Washawski and was really looking forward to working with him again also.

They planned to put the friends under Witness Protection Protocol, and hopefully it should all run smoothly.

Athos tried to call his old friend Takrannoc on the holotext, but there was no answer. Now he was worried. He was pretty sure that they had decided to make their way to Washawski's resistance army on their own. He knew Takrannoc that well.

"But Xenides and his henchmen are sure to follow them. He has informers everywhere. No wonder it has been almost impossible to pin anything on him," he said to Rennnik. He got in touch with Pander Tran, and he and his men made plans to follow Takrannoc and his friends to the compound. Witness Protection would have to wait. "We'll worry about that if they survive!" he said to Tran as they rushed out the door.

TWELVE

WARSHAWSKI'S COMPOUND

Takrannoc, Alex, Miranda and co. had made it to Washawski's compound without incident. He was very pleased to see them and relieved that they were safe. But no doubt Quossack and his henchmen would not be far behind. "No problem. Let them come. We'll be ready for them."

Xenides was absolutely furious when Quossack reported that Takrannoc and his friends had flown the coup. His informers had told him that they had probably gone to Washawski's compound, as Takrannoc was an old friend of his.

"How could such gross incompetence occurred?" Xenides exploded at Quossack. "Get over there and take care of this," he admonished the hitman.

"Consider it done," the assassin replied confidently.

"That's what you always say, but nothing ever gets done, Quossack. If you can't do the job, I'll find someone who can!"

Quossack left shamefaced, determined to do his job well. He called someone on the holotext.

Alex and Miranda set about telling Washawski all that had taken place – the assassinations, the break-in and ransacking. Washawski was not surprised. Nothing surprised him anymore. "Xenides has probably had you followed by his henchmen. He will stop at nothing to catch his quarry and dispatch of you quickly and efficiently."

"We're ready for a fight!" replied Takrannoc. "We'll do whatever it takes to protect the future of the people of Trixis and the other endangered planets."

"Xenides must not be allowed to get away with the deaths of thousands of innocent beings, who are just going about the business of leading their daily lives!" Alex said fervently.

"Well right now we need to get some food into you." said Washawski, You must all be starving after your long journey here."

The next day they began to fortify the Compound. The atmosphere was alive with adrenalin. Everyone just wanted the whole thing to be over. Washawski was looking forward to taking Xenides and his henchmen down, although he was sure Xenides himself wouldn't show up.

"He does all his killing from a distance, not face to face like men of honour do," he said to Takrannoc who agreed with him saying, "There is no honour with that cur."

Alex and Miranda tried to get in touch with Uuffi on Trixis to let him know that they were safe, but the holotext refused to work; nothing was going through. They were now cut off from any communication from outside the compound.

All they could do was wait for Quossack and his henchmen to appear.

Day turned into night. They took turns in grabbing as much sleep as they could.

"People like Quossack usually like to attack well after midnight," Washawski advised the friends. "When he hopes his enemy will be least alert."

"We'll be ready for them!" said Alexis and Talauris, as they both positioned themselves for the first watch.

Then it happened. The night sky, was suddenly lit up with the light of incendiary guns. The sound was deafening, as they rend the air. A few of Washawski's men were hit and ashes fell from the turrets of the compound. But there was no time for anyone to dwell on this, as they were sure that Quossack and his henchmen were edging closer and closer from the forest to the fortification. Warshawski and his men fired back. They managed to hit quite a few of Quossack's men who disappeared in a cloud of ashes.

Although the friends were very frightened, they wouldn't admit this to anyone never mind themselves. They were being kept busy keeping Quossack's men at bay, and tending to a few of Warshawski's men who had managed to escape with major burns.

Some of Quossack's men had broken through, and were climbing the compound walls. Hand to hand fighting ensued. More men on both sides were incinerated. The carnage was horrifying to the friends who, after all, were just office workers who had never fought a battle in their lives. But now they fought well. Washawski was proud to have them at his side, and told them so, adding, "I couldn't have chosen better warriors to fight with me than I have in you," he said proudly.

"We wouldn't have missed it for the world," Alexi said

with fervor, although he was actually very disturbed by all the carnage taking place.

The girls helping to keep the enemy in check, fought alongside the female resistance fighters, and also helped to tend the wounded, even though they had no nursing experience or experience with severe burns or battle.

"Well done girls!" the other female resistance girls frequently called as they all fought together, and when they were tending the wounded the nurses told them, "Just do the best you can. That's all anyone can do for them I'm afraid."

The deadly battle continued, and more carnage occurred, with losses on both sides, but still the battle raged on.

"We musn't give up!" called out Washawski from the battlements of the compound. "Help will arrive soon!" He turned back to fire at more of Quossack's men who had entered the compound, felling them with his incendiary gun, but unfortunately received a bad burn to his right shoulder.

Alexis and Takrannoc were also firing madly into the smoked-filled compound, trying to stop Quossack's men advancing any further.

When all seemed lost for Washawski and his fighters, Athos, Pander and their men arrived just in time in their police shuttle. They were fresh and ready for a fight. "Looks like we've arrived just in time!" yelled Athos to Washawski, as he and Pander and his men surrounded the compound.

"You can say that again!" Rennik called out as he rushed into the fray.

Quossack's army was soon depleted, and didn't stand a chance against Athos and Pander's men. The battle was over very quickly, with many of Quossack's men being taken prisoner.

Washawski, being treated for his burns, was very relieved

to see Athos and Pander and their men. He would rather have beaten Quossack on his own though, and told them so.

Athos just laughed at the old soldier, saying, "You probably could have done it with just your own men, I have no doubt, Washawski, but we thought we'd give you a bit of a hand with it all!" Then Washawski laughed, relieved that his Comrades in arms had not been seriously injured in the battle.

But now, however, it was imperative that Xenides was found and brought to justice. Quossack had managed to escape and was making his way back to where Xenides, where was hiding out in fear for his life. He would not give up without a fight, however, and told this to Quossack by holotext. He upbraided the assassin for "failing me yet again. Quossack was furious. 'It's time for this old man to go,' he thought.

✷ ✷ ✷

Athos received a very strange holotext: "If you want to find Xenides, he's holed up in one of his old factories on Iltium." The detective and Rennik wasted no time heading over there, where after an intensive shoot- out Exenides was successfully apprehended. The old man realized that he had been ratted out by Quossack, and vowed revenge. "I knew I shouldn't have trusted a boy to do a man's job!" he said in exasperation, as he was led off to be indicted for all his crimes.

✷ ✷ ✷

Meanwhile, Alex and Miranda and friends headed back on the civilian shuttle to Trixis, to let everyone know that they were safe, and to tell them about the battle and the outcome.

Uuffi, his wife and the islanders were very happy to hear of this, and began to celeberate accordingly. "Thank the gods that you are all safe," he said enveloping Wandana in a huge bear hug.

"I'm so glad it's all over. Now we can live in peace and quiet," added his wife, also grabbing her daughter in a warm embrace.

Alexi took his opportunity and pulled Miranda into his arms, kissing her fervently. She, without even thinking, kissed him back just as fervently.

"Perhaps there is hope for those two after all," said Wandana to her new friends mischievously. They laughed out loud.

A few days later a succession of good news came out. After an intensive battle, the elusive Xenides had been wounded and apprehended at last. Quossack and the remainder of his henchmen had also been arrested. And, in a surprising turn of events, a cure had been found by the Wandaggi for Neuroplasmosis, in a plant on Trixis, that had almost been exterminated through the fall-out from Xenides' missiles, but had miraculously survived. The scientists had already begun working on a serum that could be taken orally. A rumour had gone around that Xenides himself had financed this research, but this was later found to be a fallacy. The sense of irony where this was all concerned, was not lost on the friends and the people of Trixis, who celebrated well into the night.

For tomorrow would be a new beginning…

ACKNOWLEDGEMENTS

I would like to sincerely thank Helene Richards and Shane Tindal for the editing of this novel, and for their support and encouragement with my writing.

My family has played no small part in bringing this work to fruition: My son Simon, who kindly gave of his time and talent to illustrate and design the cover. My daughter Sarah, who helped me to understand the various facets of computer use. I shall be forever grateful for their support: and last, but by no means least I thank my husband John, who took the time to read this novel, and give recommendations and support with my writing of *Zanatek*

ABOUT THE AUTHOR

Barbara-Ann McCarthy is married with two children and one grandchild. She lives in Townsville, Queensland with her husband.

She has written short stories and poetry for many years, but this is her first attempt at a longer work. Barbara has had some stories and poems published on a Canadian Writing website, and a few short stories and a poem published in an anthology: Together We Write, Volume 7, in Australia in 2018.

Printed in the United States
By Bookmasters